THE TALE OF
CHRISTMAS STEVE

by Rich Berra

ISBN: 978-0-578-19793-7

Front and interior images by Design Art Studio

Edited by Stacey Kole

Printed and bound in the USA

First printing November 2017

Published by Branded Pros

2040 S. Alma School Rd. #1-171

Chandler, AZ 85286

www.BrandedPros.com

For information about special discounts available for bulk purchases, sales promotions, fundraising and educational needs, contact info@brandedpros.com.

Learn more about Christmas Steve at www.ChristmasSteve.org.

For Joe, Audrey and Christopher —

May you tuck the magic of Christmas deep in your hearts,

and never get too old for fairy tales.

Did you ever hear of that one fateful year,

When the night before Christmas nearly didn't get here?

Our tale starts in a room in a super big city,

Where a small elf named Steve was humming a ditty.

But it wasn't for Christmas or Flag Day or Hannukah,

There were no songs for birthdays or Thanksgiving or Kwanzaa.

No gifts and no presents, it was such a huge bummer,

No stockings in winter or fireworks in summer.

See, they didn't have holidays 'round Steve's neighborhood,
Instead they just played and made toys out of wood.
Now Steve was quite good at carving wagons and cars,
He carved trains and aardvarks and spaceships with stars.
He made very cool racetracks and super fast planes,
He carved crazy-eyed dolls with real scary names.
Steve made fire trucks and screwdrivers and non-edible wood bagels,
He made good guys and bad guys and rip-offs of Legos.
He wondered to himself, who would play with these toys?
For they were perfectly suited for good girls and boys.

Steve knew about Christmas from studying books,

He even put up a wreath in his own little nook.

But living alone in a tree felt so wrong,

His inner elf beckoned, a tug all along.

Sure, he didn't know much but he loved what he knew,

At night he would dream that his wish would come true.

Steve thought about Christmas all alone in his room,

His toys had to get to the North Pole, and soon.

But Steve was an elf, only 1-foot-3 tall,

Which even by elf standards is particularly small.

Could Christmas care to find him, truly being so short,

Did Steve even make it into Santa's report?

The one that tells Santa who's nice and who's naughty,

Those kids who were sweet — not remotely big-shotty.

Steve knew he'd love Christmas, right down to the Yule logs,

And planned to spend it alone with his two little dogs.

Penny and Jango were two snow-white poodles,

They loved Christmas time too — oh, and fresh Asian noodles.

The dogs never barked, no, not one little yap,

They'd look out the window or take a long nap.

But each year around Christmas something in them would change,

They'd hear bells or smell cookies and act perfectly strange.

They'd bark and they'd run and shake their fluffed tails,

They'd yelp and they'd yowl and go right off the rails.

Now Steve had to wonder about his dogs and their growlings,

Might they be snow dogs? You could hear in their howlings.

Snow dogs are pups that in the first of the Season,

Take off for the winter, for no real good reason.

They come back around New Year in time for some spritzer,

But their owners all wonder where they scurry to each winter.

Legend says they travel straight to the North Pole,

And when you hear those dogs barking, it's high time to go.

All white dogs are snow dogs — in case you weren't savvy,

They're workers for Santa, placed all through the valleys.

They live in Russia and Denmark and in Transylvania,

They're in Iceland and Rome and in spots I can't name ya.

They are all shapes and sizes but like the drummer boy drumming,

When snow dogs start barking, brother, Christmas is coming.

Steve jumped on Penny and she raced through the front door,

She ran through the streets like it was hardly a chore.

She went right through Missouri as quick as a flash,

Then straight up through Iowa and Michigan passed.

Past Canada they swept — all hard-frozen too,

Then Steve felt the chill only the North Pole could do.

The winter got stronger and the ice looked like silver,

Without proper elf snow gear, poor Steve got a shiver.

He hopped off his dog and saw a faint bit of light,

Was that Santa's workshop? He thought with delight.

It smelled pretty good like something was cooking,

He hoped it was strudel, not some nasty fig pudding.

As he got closer he heard some really cool sounds,

Were those toys being made and elves getting down?

They were dancing to Beyoncé and Earth, Wind and Fire,

Stacking up gifts ever higher and higher.

He walked up and knocked shyly on Santa's front door,

An elf opened it up and looked down to the floor.

There was small Steve, all of 1-foot-3 inches,

The elf towered over him and broke into stitches.

Then other elves started to hoot and to holler,

Steve felt so left out — man, why did he bother?

Here's yet another place he just didn't fit,

And Steve didn't like it — not one little bit.

They all stood around with their toy makers and sweets,
And Steve wanted to turn and go back to the street.
Some elves were dismissive and mean and it floored him,
But most just looked past him — just sort of ignored him.
He started to cry and walk slowly away,
And then at that moment, he heard a big deep voice say:

Hello, Christmas Steve, I've been waiting so long,
Please fix up some Yule stuff that's gone terribly wrong.
It's all up to you to make Christmas Eve happen,
If you do not help, the Elves just should stop wrapping.

The gifts that they made are all plastic and fake,

There's no soul in them, Steve, and that's quite a mistake.

Let me give you some background so you know the whole story,

People just hear my name and assume it's all glory.

Yes, I soar with the reindeer, no need for a horse,

It's fun to fly through forbidden airspace of course.

Sure, I have VIP clearance over Area 51,

But some of these gifts can get pretty hum-drum.

When all the kids want are electronic contraptions,

For me it's like watching a film without captions.

So I turn to the elves for some joy and some cheer,
But something's not right and I'm starting to fear.
We have some elves that make dolls and some that make candy,
Some fix flat tires, which comes in pretty handy.
Some elves like to play games, and some like to make snow.
Some Elves are elitists — it's all who ya know.
I have elves that make snowstorms and elves that make dreaming,
But somewhere they've lost sight of all Christmas's meaning.

We have so many tools, and robots on shifts,

The WRAPATRON 2000 wraps thousands of gifts.

They get bowed and slapped in my turbo-charged sleigh,

With GPS tracking to arrive Christmas day.

Yet where is the passion and the love anyway?

As Santa I must stop things from going on in this way.

So, Steve, I am making you my head Christmas Elf,

You are the last tiny helper who doesn't think of himself.

We need your own special magic and good forward thinking.

To stop Christmas from being all lifeless and stinking.

Make the holiday bright, make it overrun with some love,

From the 10 lords a leaping and the last turtle dove.

Oh yeah, Christmas Steve, we should also have fireworks,
Not just 'cause they're cool, but to celebrate our quirks.
See everyone is special and comes in all different sizes,
Some of the smallest I know are the biggest surprises.
Maybe the elves thought they could judge a wee stranger,
But they forgot about that baby born in a manger.
He didn't have much, just the love of his maker,
And Jesus grew to be quite the mover and shaker.

That's all that Steve needed to hear to get going,
He got right to work even though it was snowing.
Christmas Steve rose to the gig like an elf on a mission.
He was such a big deal, all the elves stopped to listen.

When they all stopped their judging, the season felt great,

They got ready for Christmas and went to ice skate.

The elves helped him out and started fresh from ground zero,

They went back to the basics and Christmas Steve was the hero!

Santa just watched with a smile on his face,

It was just what was needed to put things in their place.

So if this year you get gifts without batteries or plugs,

And not hooked up by bluetooth, or some social media drug.

If something's simple and honest and comes on Christmas Eve,

Chances are high, it's from Christmas Steve.

THE END